SAM THE MAGIC GENIE

SAM THE MAGIC GENIE

think about what you want,
not what you fear

BRIAN MAYNE

LONDON

1 3 5 7 9 10 8 6 4 2

Copyright © 2003 Brian Mayne

First published in the United Kingdom in 2001 by L.I.F.T. International
This edition published in 2003 by Vermilion,
an imprint of Ebury Press
Random House UK Limited
Random House
20 Vauxhall Bridge Road
London SW1V 2SA

Random House Australia (Pty) Limited
20 Alfred Street, Milsons Point, Sydney,
New South Wales 2061, Australia

Random House New Zealand Limited
18 Poland Road, Glenfield,
Auckland 10, New Zealand

Random House (Pty) Limited
Endulini, 5A Jubilee Road, Parktown 2193, South Africa

Random House UK Limited Reg. No. 954009
www.randomhouse.co.uk
Papers used by Vermilion are natural, recyclable products
made from wood grown in sustainable forests.

A CIP catalogue record is available for this
book from the British Library.

ISBN: 0 09 188945 6

Typeset by seagulls

Printed and bound in Great Britain by
Bookmarque Ltd, Croydon, Surrey

This book is dedicated

to my own daughter Shanti

and to all the children of the world

wherever they may be, and of whatever age.

It is dedicated to those who are in touch with children,

and to anyone who is still in touch with the child they once were.

ACKNOWLEDGEMENTS

I would like to thank my loving family and all those who have reached out to me, supported me, guided me and believed in me.

With special thanks to Sangeeta, my wife, for her invaluable input, advice, understanding and love, and to Dawn Fozard for her editing and input. Thank you all, without you this story would never have been told.

Contents

Preface

Writing this book has been a great pleasure. It has afforded me an opportunity to share a gift that has transformed my own life helping me to create a more magical, meaningful and wonderful life.

I was first presented with this gift when I was about thirty years of age. It arrived when my life was at a very low point. My business had crashed owing close to a million pounds, my home and belongings had been repossessed and my marriage had broken down. But perhaps the thing that frightened me the most was that I had left school early with no qualifications and had never learned to read and write properly.

My path ahead was looking very bleak, then one day I met a man who helped me to steer my life in a new direction. His message was simple: *'if you think you can, you can, and if you think you can't, you can't.'* I accepted this simple but profound truth, and along with other wisdoms that he shared as part of his gift, I began to apply it to every aspect of my life. I quickly noticed the difference it made.

It took me nearly one year to build up my belief in myself and achieve my main goal of learning to read and write well by overcoming my dyslexia. This gave me a fantastic boost in self-esteem and genuine confidence. And, although I have gone on to use the same techniques and wisdoms to achieve many other things in my life, the greatest prize has been the wisdom itself. It is the wisdom of how you can become, do, or achieve anything you truly desire. It is the wisdom that creates the foundations on which to build a life of true and lasting happiness.

It is my sincere wish that these wisdoms and truths now serve you in whatever way you choose, whether that is to build your own self-belief and confidence, achieve your physical goals, or simply create a little more happiness and peace in your life.

May you enjoy reading this story as much as I have enjoyed writing it.

Brian Mayne

2003

1. Joseph

It was late into the night, the room was dark and a young boy called Joseph lay curled on his bed gently crying. With his knees tucked tightly up into his chest and his arms wrapped around himself in a cuddle, soft tears rolled down his quivering cheek to splash upon a soggy pillow. It was not a bitter sobbing, just a gentle stream of liquid sadness, trickling from a deep pool of inner hurt.

For as long as Joseph could remember, he had felt a sort of emptiness deep inside him. Some days were better than others and there were times when he was really happy, but always deep down there was this feeling of sadness.

He had a mother and a father who were good to him. He lived in a nice home. He had lots of toys, plenty of friends and a best mate called Bob. In fact it would seem that

Joseph had every reason to be happy, but he wasn't happy. He felt sad. The one thing that Joseph really wanted, above anything else, was to be with his parents more. He loved them so very much, they were at the centre of his world, but they were always so busy. Busy working. Busy shopping. Busy talking. They never seemed to have enough time to be with him any more. When his parents went out he was normally told to stay in, unless of course they wanted to show him off. And when they stayed in, he was often asked to go out: 'Run along and play dear', 'Not now I'm busy', 'Go to your room'. Most of the time he felt alone. Even when his parents were nearby, they weren't really with him.

It hadn't always been this way. As he lay there watching the pictures of his past flash across the viewing screen of his mind, Joseph remembered a time when he was very small. He remembered times when both his parents, with smiling faces, would look so adoringly into his eyes that it seemed to touch something deep down inside him. This always made Joseph feel safe. It made him feel secure. It made him feel happy and special because, deep down in his heart, it made Joseph feel loved.

Sadly, as Joseph had grown older, his parents had looked into his eyes less and less. 'Now,' thought Joseph, 'the only time that they stare into my eyes is when they are angry with me – their faces are no longer smiling, their eyes don't sparkle and it doesn't make me feel the same way. I try to get their attention and feel their love, I show them the things that I can do and am proud of, but they are always too busy to really notice. They say things like, "That's quite good Joseph", or, "Yes, very nice dear", but their eyes are not looking into mine as they speak. Their faces are blank and they continue to stare at the television or newspaper instead.'

Joseph had noticed that his parents only seemed to love him when he had done something better than someone else. They were always comparing him to other people, measuring him against tests. They wanted him to be the best at everything. And no matter how well he had done, they always knew someone else that he must live up to, another test to pass, so that they could boast and brag about it to everyone. Sometimes it made Joseph feel like just another one of their many possessions, like a new car being displayed to the neighbours.

The pressure never seemed to stop. 'Other children manage fine,' his father would say. 'What's your problem? I expect you to be top of the class, Joseph. When I was your age I didn't have time to study at school. I was too busy helping your grandparents make a living. I want you to be well-educated whatever it costs, but you must try harder, and remember, big boys don't cry.'

It was the same with his mother. 'Really, Joseph,' she had said the other day while dressing for the office, 'if you're not the best, you're nobody and we don't like nobodys. If you want me to be proud of you, then you simply must do better.'

The final straw had come earlier that evening. Mum had stayed too late checking on people at work, and Dad had been glued to the computer screen for hours checking the price of his shares. 'Oh my God,' she had shouted when she finally burst through the front door in a fluster. 'You're not even dressed yet!' she shouted at Joseph's dad, snapping him out of his trance. 'The Grisley-Granges are coming to dinner. They're arriving in an hour, and you've done nothing. Well, I'm not giving them the satisfaction of telling people that we aren't top class. Joseph I need you to go straight to your room right now and stay there until morning. These are very important people and mummy and daddy need to make a good impression. I haven't the time to do your dinner now, but I'll bring you a sandwich later. Up you go now and study.'

He found the study hard, it was always hard when he

felt this upset. A dozen times or more he had picked up his science book, but through tearful eyes, and sad thoughts, the words on the page all seemed a jumble. 'What's the use,' his head seemed to be saying. 'You're not good enough.' His focus kept drifting back to how empty he felt. Empty in the stomach and empty in the heart. Mum had forgotten his sandwich and, worst of all, there had not even been a kiss goodnight.

So he had abandoned the book and lain on his bed wondering whether the feeling he had of not being good enough, of being worth less than other people, was causing his deep sadness. Another cold tear dripped from the end of his eyelash and splashed onto his already wet cheek. He sniffed. A shiver ran through his body and, giving a big stretch, he breathed in so deeply that it seemed to fill his whole inside right down to his toes. As he breathed out with a sigh, his breath kissed his heart and carried with it a wish. A wish to feel happy, a wish to feel protected, a wish for true love from his parents, unconditionally.

Holding this thought he curled up in his pyjamas to give himself a hug, and snuggled the silky-edged blanket under his chin. Soon, with the rhythmic rocking of his gentle breathing his eyes grew very heavy and slowly closed. All was silent now with just the easy tick-tock of the old alarm clock that sat on the bedside table, and the distant hum of an occasional car making its way along their road. With his eyes softly closed, Joseph watched the thoughts of another day slip from his mind and begin their short journey to become part of his memory. His body felt warm and relaxed as he began to drift into the world of dreamy sleep.

Suddenly, just as he was entering the place of dreams, he became aware of a strange glow in his bedroom as if someone had lit a tiny candle. His eyes snapped open as the light suddenly burst into a flash, making a loud *whooshing* noise and ending in a lingering, ringing *ping*! Joseph sat bolt upright, too startled to even shout. He stared in amazement at the sight before him. There, hovering just above the end of his bed, sat a large, shining genie. The genie looked straight at him with huge, sparkling eyes, gave an enormous grin and said: 'You called?'

2. Joseph Meets Sam

For what seemed like the longest time Joseph sat perfectly still and speechless. With wide eyes, open mouth and in total silence, he stared at the genie in front of him. 'How strange,' he thought to himself. 'I feel quite calm – I'm not even afraid.'

The genie had a wonderful warm glow about his body. His eyes were big and bright like two dancing lights and his smiling face said *I'm your friend*. The genie sat with crossed legs on a magic carpet that was floating about two feet above the floor. He was dressed from head to toe in bright silky clothes with long pointy slippers and a large, Indian-style hat that had a big, red ruby in the centre and feathers coming out of the top.

The genie said absolutely nothing – he just sat there beaming. At last Joseph found his voice and blurted out with as much courage as he could, 'Who are you and what do you want?'

'You may call me Sam,' replied the genie in a calm, gentle voice, 'and I want whatever you want.'

'What?' said Joseph, glancing around his bedroom a little anxiously, 'you want what I want – my things?' fearing that the genie had come to take his toys.

'No,' replied Sam with a huge grin, 'your wish is my command. It is my purpose to get you whatever you want.'

Joseph sat back against his pillow feeling very excited and extremely confused. After a moment of thought he looked up at Sam and said, 'I don't understand, why have you come here?'

'I have always been here, Joseph. It is my duty to get you the things that you want. Since the very beginning I have been with you. I am the one who makes your wishes come true. Whatever you ask for is what I get for you.'

'But I don't ask for things,' said Joseph, frowning.

The genie leaned forward, looked deep into Joseph's eyes and said in a knowing voice, 'You are always asking Joseph. You ask me every time that you make a wish. And a wish is anything that you want with intensity – that means anything that you think about a lot, anything that makes you feel strong feelings, like happy or sad. If you continue to think the same thought all of the time, it becomes a wish. The more you think about it, the stronger the wish grows. Your strongest wish becomes my command and duty to make it happen for you.'

Joseph sat with a puzzled look on his face thinking about what Sam had just said. 'But I've wished for lots of things that haven't happened,' he said.

'Like what?' replied Sam.

'Well, like that new video game I wanted.'

'Yes, I was working on that wish for you Joseph, and I was about to make it happen when you started wishing for a new bike instead. Remember Joseph, it's the thing that you think about most often that becomes the strongest wish and you thought more often about riding your bike than you did about playing the video game.'

'Oh,' said Joseph, thinking about his bike. 'Hmm, yes – I did think a lot about how cool it would be riding my bike, and it *did* happen – I got one for Christmas. But there are lots of other things, things that I know I spent a really long time wishing for, and they never happened.'

'Such as?' said Sam rubbing the end of his chin.

'Well, I wished for one whole month that I wouldn't have to go and stay with Auntie Mabel.'

'Did you indeed?' replied Sam in a slow, rolling voice.

'As I recall Joseph, what you actually thought about most of the time was being at Auntie Mabel's and how horrible it would be. You thought about it often and you thought about it with strong feelings, especially the times when you imagined having to eat her home-made lemon curd pie. Your thought became a wish and then I made it happen.'

'You did what!' stuttered Joseph with a look of horror. 'You fixed it for me to go to Auntie Mabel's and eat lemon curd pie even though you knew I didn't want to?'

'You must be careful of what you spend your time thinking about Joseph. If you didn't want to go to Auntie Mabel's, then you should have thought about yourself being somewhere else instead. People always get the things that they wish for, even if they didn't really want them.'

'What?' said Joseph in surprise. 'You mean other people have genies too?'

'Everyone has a genie, Joseph. Every single person in the whole wide world has their very own special genie to help make their wishes come true. Sadly, most people are not aware of it. They may have heard that genies exist watching their thoughts and listening to their comments, then working a sort of magic to make them happen; but very few people believe that it's true, especially grown ups.'

'You see, Joseph,' continued Sam, rubbing the end of

his chin again with one hand while leaning back on the other, 'genies can only answer when they are called and the rest of the time they are kind of invisible. You have to be very still and quiet inside of your head before you can hear your genie talking to you. Most people are so busy thinking about all the things in their life that they are never really relaxed enough to hear their genie, so they don't believe that they have one. Only the people who search with an open mind find their genie, and even fewer of them know how to talk to their genie so as to tell him or her clearly what they want.'

'Wow,' said Joseph in a hushed tone, his mind boggling at the idea, 'where do you all come from?'

'I come from nowhere and everywhere; in truth Joseph, I am always present. There is an invisible link between us. In a way, you and I are part of each other. I am the part of you that carries out your wishes and you are the part that makes the wishes. You could say we are partners. One of my reasons for being is to do all the important things that you don't have time to think about. I am the part of you that tells the different organs of your body what to do. I tell your heart to beat, your stomach to digest food and your blood to circulate around your body. You never need to think about these things because it is my job to take care of them. I'm the head librarian for all of your memories. I am the silent observer of your thoughts, the listener of your words, the granter of your wishes. I am part of you, the other-than-conscious part of you, and I am always here to serve and protect you.'

Joseph felt a warm glow from his heart that made every part of him feel good as he sat and thought about being loved and protected. For some strange reason, sitting there with Sam felt like being with someone he had known for a very long time. Even though he didn't fully understand what Sam was saying, his words gave Joseph a fantastic feeling. He moved closer to the carpet and peered straight into Sam's eyes, 'If you've always been here how come I can only see you now?' he asked, in his bravest questioning voice.

'You have never wished from your heart before, Joseph. Any thought that also gives you a strong feeling is a powerful thought and will become a wish. But a wish from the heart is much more powerful than a wish from the head and tonight you made a wish from your heart. That is why I am here and you can see me now.'

There was silence again in the room. Joseph was thinking very hard about everything that Sam had told him. His head felt like it was overflowing with thoughts swirling all around. One part of his head was thinking thoughts that whispered to his fears: 'Stay away,' they said, 'beware,' they said, 'Close your eyes and shout to make it go away,' they said. Nowhere in Joseph's science book was there any mention of genies.

But the other part of his head was connected to a deep knowingness that the genie spoke truth. He had an undeniably strong feeling that there was something very special about the genie, maybe even a new friend. The thoughts that sprang from these feelings bubbled up enough confidence for Joseph to overcome his fears. Looking up at Sam he said with open curiosity, 'I want to believe you, to believe in genies, really I do. But I don't understand. My head aches from thinking, I don't know if I've ever thought so hard. And I still don't understand how you can be part of me and at the same time still be you. I want to know how it all works, especially how to tell you what I want, honestly I do. But at the moment I don't understand, I only wish I did.'

Sam took a deep breath, puffed up his chest and beamed bright with happiness. The already enormous grin on his face grew twice as large and, with a look of total delight in his dancing eyes, he reached out a friendly hand, chuckling in a soft voice, 'Your wish is my command! Trust your feelings Joseph, take my hand, and I'll take you on an adventure.'

3. The Journey Begins

Joseph peered out of wide-open eyes at the silky blackness that now surrounded him. Two very strange things had just happened. Firstly, the moment that he had touched Sam's hand there was a flash of light and he had found himself sitting on the carpet next to Sam. What's more, they were no longer in his bedroom. One minute he was sitting on his bed reaching out to take Sam's hand and the next moment he was riding on the carpet next to him. The other strange thing was that the carpet had become much larger. When Joseph had been in his bedroom it had been just the right size for one person, but now it was plenty big enough for both of them and with room to spare.

Joseph felt instantly safe on the carpet with Sam, but at the same time his heart was pounding with excitement and a little fear about everything that was happening, and where they might be going. Sam sat just behind him and when Joseph turned around to give him a grin he noticed that the glow from Sam's body seemed even brighter than before. There was also a glow around the outside of the carpet now, like a bubble of shining, clear light.

Joseph also had a bubble inside him. A bubble of curiosity and courage that shouted with excitement 'enjoy this adventure'. He bit his lip, found his confidence, and edged forward a little. Copying Sam, he sat with crossed legs and a straight back, pressed his face forwards against the rush of oncoming air and peered out into the twinkling vastness before them. Above, the night sky looked like black silky velvet, while below, a foggy cloud streamed off in all directions like a fluffy blanket. Here and there, great lightning flashes lit up areas of the cloud like giant pearl-coloured light bulbs.

'Look there!' shouted Sam, pointing to their left. A streak of bright golden light cut through the blackness, like a huge whirling firework with a golden sparkling tail and disappeared into the distance.

'Cool!' yelled Joseph wanting to jump to his feet but thinking better of it, 'a shooting star – perhaps I should make another wish!'

'Oh, that was not a star, Joseph,' said Sam very matter-of-factly, 'and now that you mention it, this isn't even the night sky.'

'What?' Joseph looked all around to try and see the moon, 'are we in outer space?' he asked, in a hushed, cautious voice, wondering whether he should begin holding his breath.

'Inner space,' replied Sam. 'We are in the space between the world of thoughts and the world of things. What you mistook as a shooting star was really a thought and we are taking the journey of a thought.'

'I didn't know that thoughts had journeys!' said Joseph turning his head to face Sam.

'In your bedroom you wished to "understand how it all works", how thoughts turn into things,' said Sam, 'and the best way to understand anything is to experience it. Therefore, we are taking a journey of discovery to somewhere very special – we're going to the inside of your head.'

Suddenly, from what seemed like out of nowhere, a huge spiralling thought came whizzing straight towards them. Tumbling and spinning, the thought blazed a trail of golden thought-dust behind it as it streaked through the blackness on a crash course with the carpet. 'Look out, it's going to hit us!' cried Joseph out loud while ducking low and placing his hands over his head.

'Think, "miss"!' Sam shouted back, as he jumped to his feet and rode the carpet like a surfboard. Digging his back heel into the carpet he swung it sharply to the left and up tightly. The thought went speeding past, just a few inches behind, like a huge sizzling comet, showering both of them with golden thought dust.

'Phew, that was close!' said Joseph. 'For a moment I thought it was going to hit us.'

'If you had continued to think that thought it would have,' replied Sam sitting back down and crossing his legs again. 'As I was saying, we are on the journey of a thought to the inside of your head. And the rules about how things happen here are a little different from the outside. Everything here takes place at the speed of thought. Whatever you think about will start to happen very quickly.'

'In the world of things,' continued Sam, brushing gold thought-dust from his shoulders, 'there can be quite a big gap of time in between thinking of something and then it happening. But in the world of thoughts, as soon as you begin to think about something it will start to happen.'

'That sounds dangerous. I might think of something bad,' said Joseph anxiously looking around himself for any more stray thoughts.

'That's possible,' answered Sam, 'but it is even more

dangerous not to know that you are making things happen with your thoughts, and in your world people do that all the time.' Joseph sat quietly trying not to think of things that he didn't want to happen.

'This is hard!' he said after a few moments of silence.

'If you think that it's hard, then hard is what it will be,' replied Sam who was looking out into the distance. 'The very best way of not thinking about something that you *don't* want to happen, Joseph, is to think about something that you *do* want to happen. You can only think about one thing at a time, good or bad, and if you are thinking about what you want there will be no room left for any thoughts about what you don't want.'

'What a brilliant idea,' said Joseph and decided to think very hard about a large double-choc-nut-chip ice-cream topped with a chocolate flake. He created a picture in his mind of how the ice-cream would look and imagined the taste and feeling of each smooth, cold mouthful. As he focused his mind on the ice-cream, a pile of golden thought-dust lifted up from the carpet and began to swirl in a circle in front of him. Faster and faster the thought-dust whirled and sparkled. Then *flash* there it was – his large double-choc-nut-chip ice-cream, complete with a flake in the top, just as he had imagined it!

Joseph let out a yell of delight, and grabbed the ice-cream with both hands. He took hold of the flake, scooped a large dollop of choc-nut-chip on to the end and opened his mouth wide. Just as he crunched his teeth down onto the heaped-up flake, Sam patted him on the back of his shoulder and shouted, 'There it is!'

'There what is?' said Joseph looking up, and the ice-cream vanished back into sparkling dust. 'My ice-cream. It's … it's gone … vanished!' cried Joseph, staring open-mouthed at where his ice-cream had been.

'Not now,' said Sam, getting to his feet, 'we're here now.' Joseph looked up again at Sam's outstretched arm which was pointing to a huge, swirling mass of thoughts spinning in a circle like a great, golden tornado.

'Wow, what's that?' gasped Joseph, forgetting all about his ice-cream.

'It's the gate,' replied Sam, 'the place where thoughts enter and leave your mind.'

As they moved closer the wind got stronger and Joseph gripped hold of the carpet. He could see that the thoughts were spiralling in a big circle, spinning round and down, round and down, and then disappearing into the misty clouds below, like water down a sink. 'Where do they all come from?' he whispered to Sam.

'That all depends on what type of thought it is, Joseph. Some thoughts, like these golden ones in front of us, are eternal thoughts. That means they are always here. Many people, from all over the world and from all times in history, have shared these thoughts. They are always ready to pop into your mind, so long as your mind is open to them. Now look carefully at the centre of the spiral and tell me what you see.'

Joseph stretched his head forward and fixed his eyes on the swirling mass, looking past the thoughts on the outside to the centre of the spiral. 'I can see other thoughts of all different colours,' he said, excitedly. 'They seem to be spinning in the opposite direction, rising from the misty cloud and circling upwards.'

'Well done,' said Sam with a big smile. 'They are another type of thought. They are the thoughts that you create yourself.'

'Really?' said Joseph, feeling quite impressed with himself. 'How do I do that?'

'You do it by thinking,' replied Sam. 'When you think, you ask yourself a question and then give yourself an answer. Each new question that you ask yourself is the birth of another thought. The coloured thoughts in the centre are some of your thoughts or questions that are leaving your mind. And the golden thoughts that are coming in are some answers and ideas to questions you have already asked. One of these thoughts will be the answer to your wish for understanding.'

Sam rose to his feet and once again began to surf the carpet while Joseph knelt at the front looking out. Closer and closer they flew towards the spinning mass of thoughts, and stronger and stronger the wind became, until finally they were so close that Joseph could almost touch them.

'That one!' cried Sam, raising his voice to be heard above the howl of the wind. 'That's the thought we want.' The huge sparkling thought went streaking past them flicking its long, golden tail behind. 'Follow that thought!' shouted Sam as he steered the carpet after it. Round and round and down and down they went. Chasing faster and faster as the circle became smaller and smaller. 'Quickly, grab its tail,' said Sam. 'We can ride it all the way in.'

Joseph gulped nervously as he reached forward with a trembling hand, while gripping tightly on to the carpet with the other, and grabbed at the end of the thought's tail.

'Got it!' he shouted triumphantly, clutching hold of the sparkling tail as the thought instantly raced off bucking and twisting like a wild animal and showering both of them with golden thought-dust as it wriggled. 'Oh! It feels really strange,' Joseph shouted back to Sam with a look of unease, 'sort of tingly-electric.'

'Yes, answer-thoughts often have a strong, excited energy,' said Sam. 'You'll be fine though, just keep hold now no matter what happens.'

Huge coloured thoughts sparkled and whirled all around them as Joseph held on to the golden thought which raced ever faster down into the centre of the tornado. 'Wow, look at that!' Joseph gasped. Right there, in the eye of the spiral, was a large opening and out of it came beams of brilliantly coloured light. 'It's like a giant dancing rainbow,' said Joseph, 'and the thought is taking us right down towards it, through the cloud.'

'As I said earlier Joseph, that is not really cloud,' Sam shouted back. 'That is the top of your mind, the world of thoughts; it's the part of you that does your thinking, and the opening is the gateway to the inside. Now, hold on tight to that thought. It's going to get a little bumpy, we're going in!'

4. Inside-Out and Outside-In

Joseph's knuckles had become stiff in his effort to hold on to the sparkling thought, as it whirled and spun around. In fact, they had been spinning round so fast that the coloured thought-clouds had all merged together to form a sort of thick multi-coloured fog in the centre of the tornado. Reds, yellows, greens, blues and all the colours you can imagine glowed and sparkled like crackling electric in the dancing beams of light.

As they corkscrewed down through the eye of the vortex and out the other side, the fog began to clear and the first thing that came into Joseph's view was the top of a huge volcano. It appeared through the clouds like a great iceberg rising out of the water. Sam, who was still surfing the carpet, steered them away from the clouds and over towards the volcano. The volcano top was silent and covered in snow with soft milky steam slowly puffing from the huge hole in the top. In the dim early morning light it felt calm, still and peaceful after the wild roller-coaster ride of the vortex. Joseph felt himself begin to breathe a little more easily and relax his grip again.

'You can let go of the thought now Joseph,' said Sam, steering the carpet out of the clouds. Joseph was able to get a much better view. He looked down the steep rocky sides of the volcano and saw that it rose up from a beautiful island surrounded by shining blue sea. There was a small town, a tiny harbour with little boats coming and going, and at the mouth of the harbour was a lighthouse, just like one Joseph had once visited on holiday. Some of the island was covered in jungle and all around the outside was a beautiful, golden sandy beach. The island reminded Joseph of a picture in his geography book at school. The more he looked at it, the more he had the strange feeling that he had been there before. Meanwhile, Sam was flying the carpet in a large circle around the top of the volcano and they passed over the lighthouse beam as it shone out into the distance. The carpet came to a stop and hovered at the volcano with the golden thought floating beside it.

'It's quite small isn't it, the world of thoughts?' said

Joseph kneeling on all fours so as to lean over the edge of the carpet and look down at the island.

'Oh, this is just your world, Joseph, your very own island of understanding,' answered Sam with a grin. 'The world of thoughts is bigger than you can imagine.'

Joseph studied the town below more closely. 'These buildings look very familiar,' he said. 'I'm sure I've seen them somewhere before! That one over there,' he pointed with his arm, 'the large grey one with the playing field, that looks like my school.'

As Joseph pointed, the lighthouse beam swung across and shone down on the building. 'Hey, it is my school!' he shouted jumping up. 'I can see it clearly now.'

He spun around to ask Sam why it was here on the island, just as a grey, puffy stray thought-cloud floated past Sam's head and drifted off into the distance. It took Joseph's attention as it wandered and bobbed in the breeze, then, suddenly he saw behind it the huge tornado of sparkling whirling thoughts that they had just passed through. It had the same funnel shape that it did on the other side, only now it was the other way up. Golden answer thoughts were spinning around and out, while other coloured question thoughts were spiralling in and disappearing up through the centre. The misty thinker-cloud stretched out in all directions, a mixture of sky blue and white with glowing coloured thoughts sticking out from it here and there. Joseph studied the cloud in total wonderment.

'When the thinker thinks, thoughts are created,' Sam explained. 'What?' puzzled Joseph, not understanding what Sam had said.

'You see there,' Sam pointed to a blob of red and yellow fizzing thought that was bulging out of the blanket of misty thinker-cloud, 'that, Joseph, is a new thought grow-ing. Each time you think the same thought the thought grows a little bigger. Eventually, the thought grows enough to float free of the thinker-cloud.'

The winds of change began to blow and the little stray thought-cloud drifted back again towards the hovering carpet. 'There are all kinds of thoughts in your head, Joseph,' Sam said, nodding at the drifting grey thought. 'This one here is a stray thought, it has no special purpose, nothing that it is meant to do. It just drifts wherever it is taken. Thoughts are like people sometimes, Joseph. If they have no purpose, mission or special thing to do, then they just drift wherever the wind blows and often feel lost.'

'Now these are very different,' continued Sam, pointing up to some coloured thoughts that were growing from the thinker-cloud. 'These have a strong purpose, Joseph. The silver cloud is a question-thought, the purple one is an idea-thought, and the red and yellow one is a change-thought.'

'I've never heard of a change-thought,' said Joseph, studying the red and yellow blob.

'Oh you know it,' chuckled Sam, 'you just may not know the name. A change-thought is a thought that helps you grow your understanding about something. Sometimes a change-thought can be a new idea or belief that you have which helps you to create a clearer picture of the outside world, here, in the inside of your head.' Sam stretched out his arms wide. 'All of this is your world, Joseph. You have created it here inside your head to help you understand the world around you outside. That,' Sam pointed upwards to the thinker-cloud, 'is where you create thoughts and ideas. And that down there,' he nodded towards the ground, 'is like raw putty without form, and waiting to be shaped. It is made from a mixture of imagi-nation dust, memory bubbles and feelings fluid. When a thought from the thinker-cloud touches the putty of form, it shapes into whatever the thought was about. Each time you think about the big world outside, you grow some new thoughts here to create and shape this little world on the inside of your head. This is your outside-in world.'

'Do you mean none of this is real?' said Joseph looking down at the school again.

'It's all real to you, Joseph. This is your very own personal copy of the outside world. Like a model, or toy-town that you have created to help you understand how everything in the big world works. You could call it your very own personal map-room.'

Joseph was still looking at the school. Children were arriving and chatting to each other in the playground. 'What did you say this is all made from?'

'Imagination dust, memory bubbles and feelings fluid,' repeated Sam.

'What? Even the people?' said Joseph who was now checking the playground carefully to see who was there.

'Everyone and everything,' replied Sam. 'Everything that has ever happened to you has helped to create your inside world. When something happens on the outside, you think about it here, in your inside world, your new thoughts grow, and then float down from the thinker-cloud. As each new thought hits the imagination dust, memory bubbles and feelings fluid, it is moulded and shaped into a copy of the thought.' Sam paused for a moment so Joseph could absorb this. Then he asked, 'Can you tell me what a car looks like, Joseph?'

'Of course,' replied Joseph, thinking about his father's car, 'It's blue, has five doors, and a wheel at each corner.'

'The reason you can tell me that is because you have a picture of your father's car in your head, Joseph. Look there,' Sam pointed down to a car exactly like the one Jospeh had just described. 'In the same way,' continued Sam, 'you have a picture or model of everything else that has happened to you.'

A whistle blew down in the playground calling the children into the school. Joseph watched two boys having the last kick of their football, just as one of them booted it a little too hard and it flew over the high fence and into the garden next door.

'That's Mrs Bagwalt's house,' gasped Joseph out loud, his eyes darting quickly to scan her garden. 'And there she is,' Joseph whispered to Sam in a hushed voice drawing back from the edge of the carpet, 'and she's a witch!'

Joseph felt a shudder of fear run through his body all the way from his toes up to the top of his head giving him goose-bumps. Everyone had always said how Mrs Bagwalt was an old witch who ate small children for dinner, and now there she was, with a big black crooked hat, just like out of a fairytale. In the playground a teacher moved the last of the children into the school while, behind the fence,

Mrs Bagwalt picked up the football, jumped onto her broomstick and flew out of her house.

'Carpets can fly faster than broomsticks, can't they?' asked Joseph in a hopeful voice.

'Why do you want to fly faster than a broomstick?' Sam answered slowly and seemingly unconcerned.

'Because she's a *witch*, and witches eat small children, and I'm a small child,' flustered Joseph, amazed that Sam didn't see the urgency of the situation.

'Have you always thought that she was a witch?' asked Sam, in the same casual tone.

'Everyone has always said that she was,' Joseph stressed anxiously, glancing over the edge of the carpet.

'Yes, but have *you* always thought that she was a witch?' asked Sam firmly. Sam's question and calmness pulled Joseph out of his panic. He closed his eyes and searched the memory pictures of his past that flickered through his mind. He remembered a time when he had been walking home from school with his friends and, like the other boys just now, he had kicked his football into Mrs Bagwalt's garden. As she opened her front door all the other children had run away, but Joseph had stayed rooted to the spot in fear, unable to speak or move, and was surprised to see that Mrs Bagwalt didn't look like a witch at all. In fact, she looked a little like his

Granny! And he was even more surprised when she smiled at him and gave him back his ball. Other memories began to flash up. More than once Joseph had seen Mrs Bagwalt smiling at him from behind her curtains as he walked to school. Yes, she was actually quite nice at those times he thought.

A very loud and sudden pop made Joseph jump and snapped him out of his memory with a jolt. The red and yellow change-thought had shot out of the thinker-cloud like a cork out of a fizzy bottle of pop and was hissing and whizzing red and yellow thought-dust as it zig-zagged through the air like a runaway balloon. Mrs Bagwalt was still flying down the road on her broomstick while the change-thought twisted and turned in a winding path as it snaked straight towards her. Then, *splat*, it hit her right on the head and she disappeared into the exploding cloud of red and yellow dust.

As the dust settled, Joseph peered down to see what had happened. 'Sh … she's changed!' Joseph exclaimed to Sam in complete amazement. 'She's different, she doesn't look like a witch any more.' Mrs Bagwalt was still travelling down the road, only now instead of flying on a broomstick she was riding her bike. And instead of being dressed like a witch with a big hat she looked like a nice old lady in a neat Sunday bonnet.

Joseph watched in silence as Mrs Bagwalt parked her bike at the front of the school, took the football from the basket and walked into the entrance. 'She's going to give the ball back isn't she?' said Joseph, nodding to himself, 'just like she did for me that day.'

'Yes,' replied Sam.

'And the thought changed her from the witch into the nice old lady?' continued Joseph.

'You changed her!' said Sam, turning to look into Joseph's eyes.

'But I saw the red and yellow thought blob whack her on the back of the head and then she was different.'

'Yes,' continued Sam with a smile, 'and you, Joseph, were the thinker of the thought. Remember this is your world. It looks the way you think it should. When you believed without question the people who told you Mrs Bagwalt was a witch, you created her here in your inside world to look like a witch. Your saw her the way you believed she was.'

'But what made the change-thought shoot out of the thinker-cloud?'

'You did!' said Sam again. 'When you remembered some of the nice things that Mrs Bagwalt had done, like smiling at you from her window, you helped the change-thought to grow a little more and break free. That thought has been growing ever since you first saw her differently – the day when she gave you your ball back.'

Mrs Bagwalt walked out of the school and got back on her bike. As Joseph watched her pedal down the road towards her home, there was a sudden flash and she turned back into the witch and then flashed again back into a nice old lady. 'Did you see that!' said Joseph. 'How mad, she just flickered from one to the other.'

'Yes,' replied Sam. 'New beliefs and ideas can take a while to settle and stick. Sometimes we need to think the same thought many times before we fully accept it as being right and true. Everyone creates their own world, Joseph. Some people create a happy world. Some people create a crazy world. And some people even create a sad world. It just depends on what thoughts you choose to think.'

'What's my world like?' Joseph thought to himself out loud. And for the first time since he had been with Sam, he felt the old deep-down sadness inside of him. A dark grey thought-cloud moved across in front of the sun. The sky became overcast and tears started to well up in Joseph's eyes.

Sam leaned forward, put his arm on Joseph's shoulder and asked in a soft gentle voice, 'Do you remember the thought that first brought me to you, Joseph? The thought you had been thinking just before I appeared in your bedroom?'

'I suppose so,' said Joseph listlessly, suddenly not feeling very enthusiastic. He closed his eyes for a few moments, 'I was wondering again about why I felt so sad and then I made a wish to feel better.'

A shimmering sound, like someone shaking a half-full coffee jar, made Joseph snap open his eyes and look up. The noise was coming from the golden answer-thought that they had followed through the tornado and was now float-ing at the front of the carpet. It was shaking and vibrating like a sparkler with a shiver, sprinkling golden thought-dust into the air. Each time it shook, the shimmering noise became louder and the thought grew a little larger.

'This is your answer-thought, Joseph. It has drawn you here to help you understand. You now know the power of thoughts and some of the answer. Are you brave enough to explore yourself further and discover the rest of the answer to why you feel sad and how to be happy? Knowing how to be happy is not something that everyone learns and it could change your life forever. You will never be the same again – are you really sure you want the answer?'

'Yes,' replied Joseph in the fraction of a moment that it had taken to listen to his heart. The answer-thought started to shake again, vibrating faster and faster this time, and then *whoosh!* it suddenly expanded like a balloon so big and fast that it completely covered the carpet with Joseph and Sam on the inside of it like a giant bubble of golden light.

'Excellent,' replied Sam with a huge grin. 'Step one was fun and now is done. Step two is all about you. Onward carpet, let the journey continue.'

5. The Tree of Self

For a few moments, as the answer-thought joined with the carpet, the light bubble wobbled about like jelly, and looking out from the inside was like looking through a crazy window of wonderful golden glass. Then, *ping*, in an instant it became perfectly still, transparent, and so fine you could hardly tell it was there. It was like a warm glow of soft light that gave everything on the outside a clean, sparkling shine.

Joseph sat on the carpet with Sam peering out, and was just about to ask 'what happens now?' when the light bubble and carpet began to shiver and quiver, slowly at first, then faster and faster. 'This feels like a car revving its engine before a race!' thought Joseph to himself. He cautiously leaned forward to grab hold of the front of the carpet and, just as his hand reached the tassels, the bubble and carpet shot off as fast as a rocket. As the carpet accelerated Joseph flew backwards and Sam quickly stretched out his arm to catch him. With Sam supporting his back, Joseph slowly strained forward against the rush of acceleration and grabbed hold of the front of the carpet with both hands.

'Thank you,' he shouted back to Sam, almost breathless, as they raced as fast as a roller-coaster, first down, then banking hard around the outside of the volcano and whizzing up the other side towards a small clearing in the trees.

The clearing was about halfway up the volcano on a large, flat area that came out from one side and then sloped gently down to the jungle below. Thick green trees grew all the way up the long slope and completely covered the flat area at the top, except for the clearing in the centre. As they came closer, they flew in a big circle and Joseph could see that the clearing formed a small and beautiful natural park. In the very centre of the park was a pond. And in the centre of the pond was a tiny island with one small tree growing out of the very middle. As the carpet slowed, they continued to circle round and slowly down, like a spiral-slide at a funfair, all the way down to skim gently across the surface of the pond and come to a stop next to the tiny island.

Joseph's knuckles were stiff again from holding on to the carpet so tightly and he was pleased to relax his grip.

He slowly rose to his feet to stretch his legs, feeling a little dizzy from the ride. He looked round at the park. Tall, leafy trees surrounded the outside with smaller ones and moss-covered rocks nearer to the pond. The water in the pond was crystal clear and seemed to be bubbling up from underground. The little tree in the centre of the island caught Joseph's attention. It was perfectly formed with its leaves packed tightly together. The whole tree seemed to sparkle and shimmer with all the colours of the rainbow.

As Joseph turned to face it he was instantly taken by its beauty. 'It's about the same height as me!' he said, his eyes not moving from it.

'Exactly,' replied Sam, 'it's your Tree of Self. As you grow, so it grows.'

'Cool!' exclaimed Joseph, not really hearing Sam, his attention still focused entirely on the tree. 'It's made from millions of tiny crystals, the leaves, branches, trunk. Everything, even the island seems to be made of crystals, and I can see a reflection of myself in all of them; it's mad, like a million tiny mirrors all showing *me*.'

'Look closer, Joseph,' said Sam with a knowing smile, 'and tell me what you see.'

Joseph stood at the very front of the carpet, with his toes almost hanging over the edge, and examined the tree carefully. 'None of the pictures is the same. Each crystal has a different picture of me, doing different things, it's like watching a million home videos at the same time!' Joseph couldn't take his eyes off the tree – it was the most enchanting thing he had ever seen. Each crystal was like a tiny television screen showing a moving picture of him at some point in his past. At the bottom of the trunk were images of when he was a baby, then when he was very young, gradually moving up the tree where the leaf at the very top was showing pictures of things he had done just yesterday.

Sam leaned forward and whispered into Joseph's ear, 'Every thought that you have ever thought is recorded here in these pictures. Every feeling you have ever felt, and every idea that you've ever imagined, all are permanently recorded here in your Tree of Self.'

'Is it sort of my memory?' Joseph questioned, his eyes still glued to the shimmering tree.

'Oh it's much more than that,' answered Sam, 'it's the part of you that helps you to be constant. The reason why you don't always need to think about who you are and how you behave, is because you have a picture here that automatically tells you. See there,' Sam pointed to a crystal leaf that was showing little moving pictures of Joseph riding his bike. 'If you want to ride your bike again tomorrow, you won't need to re-learn how to do it, because there is already a picture of you doing it before, and I can then simply make all your actions copy that picture. I do the same with all of the other pictures when you choose to do anything you've done before.'

Joseph scanned the tree with darting eyes, looking at all the different images of his past. There were pictures of everything – of him at school, of him in the playground, on holiday and at home with his parents.

Near to the school pictures was one of him walking home with a model of a dinosaur that he had made at school. He was so pleased with it. One of the legs was a little crooked and the head was a bit too big for the body, but to Joseph it was the very best dinosaur ever and the thing that pleased him most was that he had made it all by himself.

Remembering his dinosaur gave Joseph a good feeling and he felt warm as the sun started to beam through the clouds. Then he noticed the picture on the leaf directly next to it showing images of him proudly presenting it to his parents. 'Yes, that's very interesting dear,' said his mother, not taking her eyes off her laptop computer, 'but I don't think there's too much work for dinosaur creators these days. They are all extinct now you know. Why not pretend be a lawyer dear, that way you'll be preparing to follow in mummy's footsteps when you're older.'

Joseph's father was on the phone when Joseph placed his prized model in front of him and crouched on his knees waiting for his father to look into his eyes. 'Yes, Charles,' Dad was saying, 'I can't believe how the share price has fallen, I was just checking the figures, got to go now, bye.' He looked down at Joseph, 'Dinosaurs, hey. Well,' he said as he put the phone down and picked up his newspaper. 'That's all very good son, but what about your maths grades, hey, your exams are due soon and I'm expecting top marks from you, my boy,' said his dad in a stern voice, his eyes already fixed back on a column of numbers.

Standing next to the tree Joseph watched the flickering pictures and felt again how his heart had sunk when his parents hadn't really liked his dinosaur. Again he started to feel the deep-down sadness inside. The wind changed direction and a dark grey thought-cloud drifted in front of the sun. The first spots of rain fell at the same time as a fat teardrop rolled from Joseph's eyelash. 'Could be in for a downpour!' said Sam throwing up a handful of thought-dust that instantly sprang into a big umbrella. He reached out his other arm and put it gently around Joseph's shoulders.

'What makes you feel so sad, Joseph?' asked Sam, in the softest, most loving tone.

'I don't know!' said Joseph, starting to quiver and shiver a little. 'I just don't feel right. I think there must be something wrong with me. I'm not really good enough, other people always seem to be better in some way. And I try, but it's so hard.' He sniffed, blinked, and two small pools of water fell from his eyes and rolled down his cheeks. Above the umbrella, the rain started falling heavier and more dark thought-clouds gathered blocking out most of the sun.

'Your best is always good enough, and you are loved, Joseph,' said Sam, pulling him closer. 'Some people are better at showing love than others, and sometimes people forget how important it is, but always you are loved. The most important thing, Joseph, is that you learn to love your *self*.'

'What?' The thought of loving his self snapped Joseph out of his gloom. 'How do I do that?' he said sniffing his running nose and wiping away his tears, not wanting Sam to see him cry.

'You do it by thinking your very best thought about your *self*,' replied Sam, with a beaming smile. 'Try it now! Think your very best thought about yourself right now!'

'I don't know what my very best thought is,' said Joseph still sniffing a little.

'Oh that's easy,' chirped Sam, 'the best thoughts are always those that contain the most joy. Now, which of your thoughts are really joyous?'

Joseph was still for a moment, then thought about one of the images on the tree that caught his attention. 'Going on holiday!' he shouted, with the same feeling of joy that filled his inside when he thought about what a wonderful adventure he had had there.

'Yes, that was indeed a time of joy,' agreed Sam, 'and which thought in particular gives you the best feeling about that holiday?'

'Saving the cat!' said Joseph, taking a deep breath and smiling at the thought of rescuing Tigger. It happened on the first day of their holiday at the seaside. Joseph was looking out from the hotel window when he saw a cat stuck up a tree. It took ages to get his father interested enough to come outside and, with the help of the man from behind the hotel desk and a ladder from the storeroom, the cat was rescued. It was only a young kitten and Joseph decided to call it Tigger. The same day they took it to the animal shelter so it could be looked after and returned to its owner. The hotel owner said that if Joseph hadn't spotted it, the cat could have been there for days. Joseph was so pleased with his good deed that for the rest of the holiday he felt a couple of inches taller and walked like he had a big medal pinned to his chest!

A sudden flash from the tree, like someone taking a picture, snapped Joseph out of his thoughts of the past and back to the present. The flash had come from the picture of Joseph rescuing the cat and now circles were rippling out from it across all the other pictures, like dropping a pebble in a pond. Suddenly all the crystal leaves focused together, like one big crystal ball, showing one big picture of Joseph and Tigger.

The rain stopped. The clouds moved away and a sunbeam shone down on the crystal tree. 'That's better!' said Sam, taking down the thought-dust umbrella.

'What's happened?' said Joseph, turning to look directly at Sam.

'You have created a new dominant thought,' replied Sam pointing at the tree. 'Remember Joseph, I always grant your wishes. And a wish is anything that you think about a lot which gives you a strong feeling. When you first thought about your dinosaur you felt good and the sun shone! Then you thought about how sad you felt trying to show it to your parents. That brought the clouds and the rain began. Whatever you think about gives you a feeling, good or bad. By thinking about how good you felt on holiday you made the good feeling more powerful than the sad and it became your dominant thought and feeling.

'The Sun of Love is always shining, Joseph. You only need to think about your best thoughts and you will feel its warmth. Learning how to love yourself means learning how to think happy thoughts rather than sad ones.' Sam again sat in his cross-legged position. He straightened his back, took a deep breath, adjusted his hat and, glancing up at the sun, announced in a deep calm voice, 'Everything is just fine, allow yourself to shine, let us continue, Joseph, I'd like you visit a very good friend of mine.'

6. Faith and the Key to Confidence

The moment Joseph sat down beside Sam on the carpet, it and the bubble began to shake and vibrate again, like a car starting its engine. They moved off, slowly at first, round and slowly up in a corkscrew shape to hover just above the crystal tree. The bubble then began to vibrate and quiver faster and faster. 'I wish I had a seatbelt,' thought Joseph, remembering what had happened earlier, and immediately felt something firm around his waist. He looked down just in time to see some thought-dust finish knitting itself into a snug belt. As he looked up again Sam was grinning at him.

'Where now?' shouted Joseph over the shaking noise.

'Inward and onward,' replied Sam, just as the bubble gave one last shudder, faster than all the rest, then *ping!*, they shot straight down and right inside of the crystal tree.

'Wow,' gasped Joseph, trying to catch his breath, 'have we got smaller or has the tree just got a whole lot bigger?'

'Both!' shouted back Sam, and everything about them seemed stretched out like spaghetti as they raced down through the branches, into the trunk, right down to the seed, and popped out through the centre root. Then, *whoosh*, they entered into a huge stream of sparkling bubbles, like diving into a big fizzy drink.

'That was too much,' said Joseph, looking like he had been on the most intense funfair ride. All around them streamed bubbles of different sizes and colours all gently bobbing along in the current.

'This is your river of life,' Sam announced like he was introducing someone.

'A river of bubbles,' Joseph said quietly to himself, looking at the sides of the golden bubble that had formed around them. 'Where does my river flow then?' he asked Sam while undoing his seatbelt and standing up.

'That all depends on you, Joseph. This underground river flows from the source of your Tree of Self all the way to your Sea of Potential and then on to untold Islands of Possibilities. The choice is yours. You're the captain and I'm the crew, you set the direction and I'll help get us there,' said Sam rising to his feet.

Bubbles of all colours and sizes were sticking to the outside of the big golden bubble around Joseph and Sam. 'Hey, some of these bubbles have got pictures on them,' said Joseph, with his face up close to the side.

'Yes,' replied Sam, 'they are memory bubbles, all floating in feelings fluid and thought dust.'

A large wobbly memory bubble of Joseph watching a cartoon floated close and stuck to the side of the golden bubble. Joseph reached out his hand and gently placed his fingers against the inside of the golden bubble at the spot where the memory bubble had landed. Instantly he broke out into roaring laughter. 'Oh, sorry about that!' he said after a few moments of giggling, still finding it hard to speak and holding his sides from the laughter, 'I don't know what came over me!'

'Memory bubbles are also mixed with feelings fluid and thought dust,' said Sam, who was also laughing. 'When you touch on the memory you will feel again the feeling of that memory.'

'Right,' said Joseph, getting his breath and taking a slight step back so as to get a good look at which memory bubble he would feel next. 'That one,' he said out loud, and placed his fingers over a bubble showing the first day of school holidays. 'Oh, that's so good,' he said feeling again the surge of excitement that comes when school breaks up. Next to be felt was the ice-cream bubble, then that full-belly contented feeling, and one of the best was the hot bubble bath.

The hot-bath memory bubble felt so good that Joseph sank down to his knees and lay back on one elbow, just as he would in a real bath. As his whole body started to relax, he let his hand gently slide from the memory of the hot bath, and skim down the inside of the golden bubble, touching and feeling many other bubbles as it fell.

The expressions on Joseph's face changed almost as quickly as his hand passed over the different bubbles and felt the different emotions. 'Ow, what's that?' thought Joseph as he suddenly got a strange feeling of uncertainty. He looked down and saw that his hand was touching a small grey bubble. As he moved closer to the edge of the carpet he could see little pictures in the bubble of himself swimming in the sea and being afraid of the long, dark tangling seaweed.

As Joseph studied the bubble, two more bubbles, also showing pictures of Joseph being afraid, floated up from the bottom of the river and stuck to the golden bubble. Joseph's feeling of uncertainty started to turn to fear. He peered down over the side of the carpet, 'There isn't any dark weed on the riverbed is there?' he asked, in an anxious voice. Before Sam could answer the golden bubble suddenly dropped deeper down towards the bottom of the river causing bubbles and feeling fluid to splash up all around them on to the carpet. More dark heavy fear bubbles had attached themselves to the side of the golden bubble and were weighing it down.

Joseph's feeling of fear began to turn to panic, 'We're sinking deeper!' he shouted to Sam. 'I think there is weed at the bottom. We might get caught in it!' he yelled, with a look of terror on his face. More fear bubbles floated up and stuck to the others taking the golden bubble down even deeper. 'I can see black weed below!' he shouted. 'Do something Sam, please.'

Sam sat very calmly smiling at Joseph. 'Ahead the tunnel splits!' he said, nodding in front of them. 'One channel leads up to your Pool of Confidence and the other goes down into strong undercurrents and dark feelings.'

'I choose the top path!' said Joseph without any hesitation, 'make us go up.'

'You are the captain, Joseph,' replied Sam, 'you must think us up. The emotions of fear and sadness are heavier than those of love and laughter. If you want to move higher you must think and feel the lighter feelings of love and laughter.'

'But I don't feel like laughing,' said Joseph still shaking with fear at the thought of the dangerous seaweed.

'Then you should think thoughts of love and laughter,' Sam said in a calm tone, 'we are always free to think whatever thoughts we choose.'

Joseph tried hard to think of nice things, but a voice in his head kept shouting, 'Look out the seaweed's going to get you!'

'Look up,' said Sam cheerfully. 'Look up, sit up, and you will feel up. Come on, act as if you're happy, change the way you are sitting.'

Joseph straightened his back and held his head a little higher. He breathed slower and deeper, and as his eyes went upwards, he noticed a small bubble showing a picture of him rescuing Tigger. It was almost the last light bubble left.

'That's it!' said Sam, 'think about what you want, not what you fear.' As Joseph thought about Tigger he started to feel a little better, lighter. He slowly pulled his arm away from the fear bubbles and reached up to the bubble of Tigger with the warm happy feeling it was giving. Other happy bubbles began to stick to the side and Joseph felt himself and the carpet rise up a little more.

'I'm starting to feel better!' said Joseph, with a sigh of relief and a faint smile.

'Thoughts always attract other thoughts of the same type,' said Sam. 'They're a little like magnets – think about something good, and that thought will attract other good thoughts. Now remember the joy,' said Sam, nodding his head.

As Joseph began to think again about all his different adventures, a huge shining memory bubble of a visit to the Natural History Museum in London stuck to the top of the big golden bubble and lifted them up even higher into the flow of happiness and love. As the current of joy caught them, they were swept up into the top channel, swirled around and upside down as if they were on a giant water slide, then with a big gush of bubbles and feelings fluid, they suddenly splashed out of an opening in the rocks and into the Pool of Confidence.

'Oh, thank you,' said a clicking voice, 'that was just what I needed, the level of the pool was getting very low.'

'Allow me to introduce you to a friend of mine,' said Sam, 'Joseph, greet Faith.'

Joseph's mouth was open but no words come out. 'Wow,' he finally said, 'a dolphin, just like at the sealife centre, only this one can talk.'

'Oh, we can all talk!' said Faith the dolphin in a clicking voice that sounded like laughter, 'but only a few humans really seem to listen. It is very nice to meet you, Joseph,' continued Faith with a flick of her tail. 'Tell me, why are you here, and where are you going?'

'I'm on the journey of a thought,' said Joseph, proudly, 'and I'm going to find out where happiness and sadness come from. Sam's helping me.'

'Is he? That's very good. And what, may I ask dear one, have you discovered so far?' said Faith who, with so few visitors, enjoyed asking questions.

'I've learnt that thinking happy thoughts makes you feel good,' said Joseph, 'and thinking sad thoughts makes you feel sad.'

'Anything else?' asked Faith, in a searching tone.

'Yes,' replied Joseph instantly, the experience of the river still being fully with him, 'thoughts are like magnets and attract other thoughts of the same type.'

'Sharp as a shellfish,' said Faith, genuinely impressed with Joseph's confidence and wisdom. 'Yes, you're quite right – and bright. Your answers are true, but they are only two, and for me to be set free, you will discover answer number three, which as you will see, is the real key. To complete your journey, Joseph, and gain your answer, you will need to visit your Sea of Potential.'

Faith pointed down with her long bottle-shaped nose to the harbour below leading to the sea. Joseph looked out across the harbour to the town on the other side, and suddenly realised where they were. The Pool of Confidence where Faith lived stuck out from volcano side like a giant soap dish just above the harbour and opening to the Sea of Potential. He glanced behind him to his right to the opening in the rocks they had popped out of, and then up to where the clearing and his Tree of Self was. He wondered momentarily about the underground river that connected the tree to the pool, and where he might have ended up if he had taken the lower channel of the river, the one that leads to dark undercurrents. 'Don't go there', a voice seemed to say in his head so clearly that he looked round to see if anyone was talking.

It was so relaxing at the Pool of Confidence that he felt totally at ease. The sun was shining more brightly now and birds were singing somewhere in the distance. The water in the pool had a wonderful silvery glow in the bright sunlight, and as Faith swam around the sparkling water made her skin shimmer like a zillion jewels. The Pool of Confidence was formed from smooth and rounded stones, like great coloured pebbles, which went all the way around the outside. At the front they stood as tall as Joseph above the level of water in the pool, and it must have been more than twice that to the harbour directly down below.

Towards the back of the pool the stones were larger, and right at the very back where it joined the volcano side, almost hidden by its shadow, was the opening to a long dark cave that led off into the centre of the volcano.

There was a sudden splashing sound as another gush of memory bubbles and feelings fluid swirled up from the rocks and into the pool from the underground river of life along which they had just come. 'Better and better,' said Faith, in a tone that sounded like singing. 'I remember when you were young, Joseph, your river streamed with happiness from your Tree of Self. The flow of love was so great that my Pool of Confidence was always full and I could swim happily into your Sea of Potential. Lately, however, the heavy emotions of sadness and fear have taken the flow downwards and the Pool of Confidence has been low. And when the pool is low, it is so difficult for me to get over the rocks to swim in your Sea of Potential, that sometimes I don't even try.'

Joseph didn't like the thought of Faith being trapped and asked immediately, 'How can I help?'

'By helping your self,' replied Faith, flicking water over her head with her long tail. 'Listen carefully, dear. To reach your goal, you will need to pass through the Cave of Fear. Here is the key that will set you and me free. Think about things, as you want them to be! God speed, good luck, and remember my words if you ever get stuck.' Faith pressed her smiling face up into the light bubble and Joseph reached out to touch the end of her nose gently with his fingers. As he looked deep into Faith's eyes a strong feeling that everything was just fine filled his whole inside, and then, with another flick and a splash of her silvery tail, she dived below the surface and was gone.

'She'll be back,' said Sam, who had been sitting watching quietly. 'Ready to continue now?'

'Yes,' affirmed Joseph, feeling more certain and confident than ever before.

'Good,' said Sam, 'trust in me, the very best fun is still to come; keep heart Joseph, we're on the home run.'

7. The Fingers of Fear

Joseph and Sam were both sitting tall on the carpet as they floated slowly across the surface of Faith's pool and into the mouth of the cave. Joseph thought his best wish to see Faith again. Inside, the cave walls danced with flickering shadows in the silver reflection of the water. At the far end Joseph could just see a faint red glow. 'That's the glow from your Life Fire!' said Sam, knowing Joseph's thought. 'It comes from deep down in the heart of the volcano.'

A sudden moving shadow on the cave wall took Joseph's attention. 'What's that?' he said out loud, with a little shudder, his eyes darting from side to side.

'What's what?' replied Sam calmly.

'I thought I saw something move, there on the wall!' said Joseph, pointing in front of them.

'I see nothing alarming,' said Sam, 'however, I notice your arm is trembling – are you cold, Joseph?'

'No, but this place gives me the creeps a little, I don't really like it in here,' he said feeling less confident now. It was getting darker as they floated with the current away from the mouth and deeper into the centre of the cave.

After a few moments of silence Joseph looked up at Sam. 'Nothing to be afraid of in here, is there?' he questioned in his best cheery, hopeful voice.

'There is no-thing be afraid of anywhere Joseph! Understand that fear is not a *thing* – it is a feeling, and for those people who live with a feeling of fear, every "thing" and any "thing" in their life will become frightening. However, in truth, there is no "thing" at all to be afraid of.'

'But everyone I know is afraid of something,' said Joseph, glancing round from side to side as dancing shadows on the walls played tricks on his eyes. 'My friend Bob is afraid that he might get bullied at school, my mum is afraid of losing her pocket organiser, and dad is afraid of the tax man.'

'Yes,' replied Sam, 'there are many types of fear, but those are all false fears, Joseph, they are not real, they are just what those people imagine could happen to them. Real fear can be your friend,' continued Sam who had taken again to rubbing the end of his chin. 'Real fear is that feeling that you get if you stand too close to the edge of a cliff, or are about to step out into a busy road. It is a strong feeling that warns you to be careful, that there may be danger. But when you imagine that something could be bad or terrible in your future, and that thing hasn't even happened, then that is a false fear, and not the type of friend that helps.

'Remember, Joseph, we are all free to think about whatever we want, and whatever we think about gives us a feeling. Think about how bad things will be and you will feel fear and sadness. Those feelings, make it hard for you to be your best, and if you continue to think those thoughts for long enough, they become wishes and then I make them happen.'

'But you wouldn't make anything bad happen to me would you?' Joseph, asked feeling a sudden twang of despair at the thought that Sam may not really be his friend.

'Only if you wanted me to,' answered Sam. 'As I have told you, you are the captain and I am the crew. You are the one who decides what you want, and I am the one that makes it all happen. You are the wisher and I am the grantor. And a wish is anything, good or bad, happy or sad, that you think about a lot and with strong feelings. Fear is a strong feeling. Tell me, Joseph, what are you afraid of right now?'

'I'm afraid there might be monsters in this cave,' answered Joseph, in an alarmed tone.

'There are no real monsters, Joseph,' replied Sam, now leaning back on one arm. 'Fear itself is the only monster. Fear is like a monster that is always hungry and what it most likes to eat is more fear. The more you feed the fear monster, the more it wants. If you don't want to feel frightened, don't feed the fear monster by thinking more thoughts of fear.'

'You can't not fear the things that frighten you,' said Joseph in a hushed tone still looking round.

'For example?' replied Sam.

'Well,' continued Joseph, 'like not passing my maths and science tests – you *can't* not fear something as scary as that.'

'You can lose your fear and feel better about your tests in the same way as you can feel better about anything else that scares you, and that is by really listening to what your fear is telling you, thank it for letting you know, and then think your best thought about it.'

'But I have been thinking my best thought about the tests for ages – I've studied really hard, taken extra classes, and I still feel terrible.'

'Yes,' replied Sam, with a loving look. 'You've worked very hard, and done very well, you can be rightly pleased with yourself, Joseph. However, understand, the thought you have had most often is of you "not passing" your tests. You think about how terrible it will be not to be able to remember any of the answers, or how bad it will be if you fail.'

'But it will be bad and terrible if I don't pass, I'll be letting everyone down, then I'll probably have to try even harder,' said Joseph with a sigh of despair at the thought.

'Listen to your fear again, Joseph, go beyond the surface of not passing your tests, and tell me what it whispers at a deeper level.' Joseph closed his eyes and listened inwardly to the undercurrent of the fear.

'You're not good enough,' it hissed in a slow voice.

'Oh,' moaned Joseph, his eyes sprung open from the realisation. 'I'm not good enough, no matter how hard I try, I don't feel good enough to succeed. I'm useless.'

'You were born good enough,' said Sam with a knowing smile. 'It is your birthright – your natural freedom to choose to be your best you in whatever you do. Being your best, Joseph, doesn't mean you have to be "the best", better than other people. It means if you can say with hand on heart that you have given your best, then that always makes you good enough no matter what the outcome, or other people's opinions. You may not always be able to control everything that happens in your life, Joseph, but you can choose your thoughts and feelings about what happens, that is what the most powerful people in life do.

'You can feel good about your tests, Joseph, in the same way that you can feel good about your self, through thinking your very best thought. Try it now. Think your very best thought. Create a picture in your head of you doing well with your tests and being really happy with yourself for trying regardless of your score.'

'Will that make me pass them?' asked Joseph in a hopeful voice.

'It will certainly help you do much, much better,' replied Sam. 'When we feel good about ourselves we naturally create the best. Besides, you were thinking sad thoughts so much, that it was about to become a wish, and I was going to help you panic and forget most of the answers to the questions.'

Sam encouraged Joseph to practise sitting quietly with his eyes closed and imagine himself doing well in his tests. He was beginning to feel much better after listening to Sam's wisdom, about learning to like and love his self by being happier that his best is always good enough. He pictured in his mind the classroom where he knew the tests would take place, and imagined being really calm with answer-thoughts flowing to him, then jumping and shouting to celebrate giving his best in the playground afterwards. And, to make sure that the thought became a wish, and Sam got the message, he imagined his thought picture with as many vivid colours, movements and good feelings as he possibly could.

'Well done,' said Sam who had received Joseph's silent wish.

Joseph giggled as he opened his eyes, 'If this works,' he thought to himself, 'I can have some real fun.' The thought gave him a little tickle inside and he looked up at Sam with a smile, 'Feeling much better now, thanks.'

Suddenly the carpet shot off to the right, twisting sharply, and Joseph was thrown on to his back. Still lying flat he looked up just in time to see a black seaweed-covered rock, so large it was like looking up at a sky-scraper, as they brushed past and it disappeared into the darkness.

'That was close!' said Joseph, getting up off his back. He looked behind them to the cave mouth. The light from outside was now just a small white circle in the blackness, the light bubble around them glowed like golden moonlight, and the red glow from the Life Fire ahead was bigger.

'We must be past halfway now,' Joseph reasoned to himself. Again there was a surge and the current swept them off to the left and dipped down into some small rapids. 'It's getting a bit fast now,' said Joseph as water splashed up through the bubble and over the front of the carpet. 'Do you think we should go a bit higher?' he said, with water starting to lap at his ankles.

'It is what you think, Joseph, that counts most,' Sam answered back calmly.

The ceiling of the cave was getting lower all the time and random stalactites pointed down like enormous spears. Joseph thought as hard as he could about being in the space between the choppy water, and the jagged rocky cave ceiling. The amount of concentration needed to think the carpet up or down was huge. It felt like they had a long way to go still and, for the first time since being with Sam, he started to feel really worried and wondered whether the journey was worth it. He peered anxiously ahead to the Life Fire at the end of the cave. In the red glow he could just about make out the outline of two enormous jagged rocks that reached right up to the roof of the cave. 'They're right in our way,' Joseph shouted back to Sam.

'Think us off to one side then,' said Sam, peering ahead to the rocks. 'Remember Joseph, you're the captain and

I'm the crew – you must think about where you want to go before I can help it happen.'

Joseph felt a growing sense of responsibility, that he must fly the carpet and not leave it to Sam. He closed his eyes and pictured them going off to the right, he also pictured the two jagged rocks. He didn't mean to, they just sort of popped into his mind. 'How's that?' he said, opening his eyes and looking up.

'Very good,' replied Sam. 'We have moved over to the right.'

'Oh no!' shouted Joseph, the rocks had also moved and were still right in their path.

'Did you picture the rocks when you had your eyes closed?' asked Sam, in a questioning tone.

'Not on purpose,' replied Joseph, 'and I thought much more about missing them.'

'Ha! That explains it!' said Sam, rubbing his chin again. 'These are the moving Rocks of Doubt. Even a small amount of doubt in your mind will bring the rocks towards you. Have another go.'

Joseph closed his eyes again and concentrated this time on steering them off to the left, but again he also saw the rocks in his mind and, worst still, them being crushed between them. As he felt the carpet swirl off to the left he opened his eyes in hopeful anticipation just in time to see the rocks also moving over to the left with them. 'I'm no good at it, I can't do it!' Joseph despaired while slapping his hands down into his lap and hanging his head.

'You are already doing it,' replied Sam, with an encouraging smile. 'You are successful at making things happen, simply be more specific about what you really want. It is like anything else in life, Joseph, think about where you want to go, not where you fear you may end up.'

'It's hard,' replied Joseph. 'I'm trying. I know if I focus on the rocks I'll steer towards them, but they keep creeping into my mind.'

'Don't think about a pink rabbit!' said Sam abruptly.

'What?' said Joseph, his mind spun out of its thought by Sam's strange request.

'Don't think about a pink rabbit!' said Sam again. 'Don't think about a pink rabbit. Don't think about a pink rabbit. What are you thinking about?'

'A pink rabbit,' answered Joseph, blankly.

'Right,' replied Sam, 'and what's the best way of not thinking about a pink rabbit?'

'I don't know!' said Joseph, completely puzzled.

'It's to think about something else instead,' answered Sam in a happy tone. 'You can only hold one type of thought in your mind at a time, Joseph, good or bad, happy or sad. Think about where you want to go. Quickly now, the current's moving faster and we're getting very close.'

Joseph closed his eyes once more. He thought with as much colour, feeling and movement as he could, only this time, instead of picturing him and Sam trying to get past the rocks, he understood what he really wanted, and imagined them arriving at the end of the tunnel.

'Well done!' shouted Sam, 'it's working, keep going.'

Joseph kept his eyes shut tight and repeated over and over to himself, 'We're at the end of the tunnel, we're at the end of the tunnel, we're at the end of the tunnel.' The carpet suddenly surged forward with a tremendous *whoosh* and, as Joseph looked up, the two towering rocks slipped by either side and they sped straight through the middle. 'Thank goodness that's over,' he said with a huge sigh of relief, but turning back round to the front, his brief moment of happiness faded.

There, right in front of them, was a giant set of stone fingers blocking their path out of the cave and up the centre of the volcano to the open air. Before Joseph even had time to ask Sam what was happening, they had run right into them and were being pressed up tight by the strong current. Memory bubbles and feelings fluid splashed up over them like a wave against a seawall as the liquid gushed out between the stone fingers and down into the bottom of the volcano to be turned into steam by the hot Life Fire.

'We're trapped!' shouted Joseph while wiping his eyes and looking down at the burning red glow from the Life Fire beneath them. Steam was rising, the light bubble gave little protection and it was getting very hot and wet. 'There's no way out, we're stuck here,' he groaned, looking to Sam for hope.

'Yes, and no,' replied Sam who seemed to be totally unconcerned by anything. 'Yes, we are stuck, but no we are not trapped – there is a way out.'

'Where?' said Joseph glancing round frantically. He was now completely soaked from waves splashing up over the carpet.

'Straight up,' replied Sam looking above them at the tunnel that led to the top of the volcano.

'But the fingers are blocking us from getting out,' Joseph shouted, totally unimpressed.

'Yes,' answered Sam, 'at present, but you can open them. These are the Fingers of Fear, and if you want to get out, you must master your fear. Otherwise we are destined to stay here until we are evaporated by the heat of the Life Fire.'

Joseph gulped at the idea of being evaporated as he closed his eyes and thought so hard about the fingers opening that it felt like his head was growing. 'I want the fingers to open, I want the fingers to open,' he said over and over to himself. A loud cracking noise, like rocks snapping, caused him to look up. The fingers had opened, but it wasn't even enough to get his head through, let alone the carpet.

'Again,' said Sam, 'and this time, say your thought out loud – it is always more powerful when you speak aloud what you are thinking.'

Joseph closed his eyes again, took a deep breath, and said out loud, 'I want the fingers to open, I want the fingers to open.' Again there was a loud cracking sound, and again Joseph opened his eyes in hope, only to see that although the fingers had opened some more, it was still not enough to get out. 'It's not working!' he cried, feeling the heat from the Life Fire, as scalding steam swirled all around them. 'What do I do? What do I do?' he shouted frantically.

'Firstly honour your fear Joseph, thank it for warning you. It is OK to feel afraid when there is genuine danger,' said Sam, calmly and reassuringly. 'Most importantly of all, remember the wisdom Faith shared with you at her pool, "the key to confidence, that will set you free, is to see and say things as you want them to be". See and say it, as if you have already succeeded.'

'I've got it!' shouted Joseph at the top of his voice with a huge shining grin. He closed his eyes, breathed in slowly all the way down to his tummy, told his self he felt calm, and then in his best, I-am-really-certain voice, shouted out loud: 'The fingers are open!' A deafening crack, so loud that Joseph had to cover his ears, came at the same time as he felt the bubble going up, like being in a very noisy, wobbly elevator.

'Well done!' shouted Sam, slapping him on his back. Joseph opened his eyes to see the open stone fingers disappearing below as they rose up quickly with the steam of the volcano. He sat down opposite Sam feeling a little shaky still but extremely alive. He had done it. He had saved them. He looked over at Sam and smiled the smile that can only come from someone who has faced fear, and chosen to be brave. A smile that flows from knowing you can succeed.

Sam recognised Joseph's smile and nodded in agreement. 'You've learnt a lot my dearest friend, when you can explain it to me, we'll be at our journey's end.'

8. A Ray of Enlightenment

As the carpet rose up the tunnel, pushed up by the puffing steam from the Life Fire, Joseph's mind raced with thoughts about everything he had learned. He repeated over and over the riddle Faith had given to him – 'The key to setting you free, is to see things as you want them to be'. Suddenly all the thoughts came together into one, like jigsaw pieces making a picture. 'That's it!' he shouted with excitement, just as they reached the top of the volcano. 'I can always be happy by choosing which thoughts I think about. Even if I can't always change what's happening, I can choose how I feel about it, and that means I can be happy about anything, for any reason.'

Joseph positively beamed with joy at his new realisation, and the big golden light bubble around them popped, sending a shower of golden thought-dust shimmering through the air. The winds of change blew. Some stray thought-clouds parted, and a Ray of Enlightenment shone down on Joseph from the Sun of Love.

The carpet gently floated over the rim of the volcano and swooshed down the side on a rolling cushion of steam all the way to the harbour below. Joseph and Sam swept down the volcano side, like snowboarders gliding down a ski slope, they skimmed over the water like a frisbee and come to a hovering stop in the centre of the harbour.

Joseph turned to Sam and gave a huge happy smile. He took a deep breath in through his nose, all the way down to his tummy, and then let it out slowly through his mouth. 'I think I understand,' he said, looking directly into Sam's eyes.

'Yes,' beamed Sam, with a clap of his hands. 'Well done, you can be rightly pleased with yourself, Joseph. This wisdom can serve you for the rest of your life, in anything that you desire. The whole universe is like a big dream machine waiting to grant your wishes and create your imagination. My last important question to you is this. Now that you know you are creating your world with the thoughts that you think, what will you choose to think about?'

'Good things!' answered Joseph, without any hesitation, 'I will choose to think about good things, things that make me happy.'

'Yes,' replied Sam, with a smile, 'it's good to think about things being good. But what thoughts do you now choose to think about your self?'

Joseph fell silent and stared blankly down into his lap as he checked his inner thoughts and feelings. 'I'll think about being my best, I'll listen to my feelings and remember that I'm good enough, but most of all, I'm going to concentrate on what I like about my self,' he said with certainty, looking up at Sam.

'Remember Faith's key,' replied Sam softly. 'See and say things as you want them to be.'

'Right,' nodded Joseph, in a quiet voice, the thought bringing a smile to his face, 'I remember. I Like My Self,' he declared in a firm tone. The sound of splashing came from behind them. Faith was leaping high into the air with excitement, and a great gush of happy bubbles was pouring into her Pool of Confidence.

Joseph had a flash of inspiration – could he raise the level of Faith's pool to set her free and send her swimming into the beautiful blue sea? 'I Like My Self,' said Joseph again, this time with more feeling, his eyes fixed on the pool just across the harbour. Another burst of good feelings bubbles flooded into the Pool of Confidence from the underground stream of the Tree of Self, and Faith's happy clicking voice sang out in appreciation.

'I Like My Self. I Like My Self!' shouted Joseph at the top of his voice and with joy in his heart, as the level in the Pool of Confidence rose higher and higher.

A deep feeling of warmth and contentment, like a belly-full of hot porridge on a cold winter's morning, swept over him and kissed his heart. 'I Love My Self!' he said in a soft, slow voice, as a single fat tear of happiness rolled down his cheek.

A great flood of happy feelings fluid gushed into the Pool of Confidence. The pool was full to the brim, then it suddenly overflowed into the harbour just below and, with one great majestic leap, Faith dived free to swim into the Sea of Potential. Joseph's heart felt like it had leapt as high as Faith at the sight of her being free. She soared through the air and into the water with a graceful ease and, with just a few flicks of her powerful tail, Faith appeared at the side of the carpet with her head poking above the waves. 'Thank you,' she said in her happy clicking voice, looking deep into Joseph eyes. 'By speaking the magic words you have set us both free.'

'I Love My Self,' Joseph whispered, fully feeling an

inner warmth and safety he had never known before, 'I love myself and I love you.'

A gurgling stream of bubbles broke the water surface just in front of the carpet and a shimmering thought-cloud drifted down from above. As Joseph watched in silence a small and beautiful sailing boat rose up from the bubbling Sea of Potential to bob merrily on top of the rippling waves.

'This is your boat named Ability which sails on the Sea of Potential,' said Sam with a smile. 'It is steered by the rudder of your beliefs, and flows with the currents of happiness.'

A fresh wind blew, filling the sails of the little boat and starting it on its journey across the Sea of Potential, to the many islands of possibilities.

'Now, it's time for us to be leaving too,' said Sam looking lovingly at Joseph. Faith gently wriggled her tail so as to stand up out of the water and kiss Joseph tenderly on the nose.

'Remember my key and the magic words of freedom Joseph. Repeat them any time you want to feel the warmth of love and happiness.'

'I'll say them every day,' said Joseph with the ring of promise in his voice.

'Good,' replied Faith, 'then my Pool of Confidence will always be full, and you and I will be free.'

The carpet slowly rose and moved away as Joseph continued to wave goodbye to Faith. 'She'll be just fine now,' said Sam softly touching Joseph's shoulder. Turning to face Sam he noticed that the Sun of Love was shining more brilliantly than ever and the people in the town also seemed happier and brighter. 'You are brighter and lighter too,' said Sam reading Joseph's thought.

There was now a light glow around the outside of Joseph, just like Sam, and a warm glow inside of him coming from the love he now felt for himself. 'I don't really want to go,' he said, looking into Sam's sparkling eyes. 'I might not ever see you again.'

'Be brave,' replied Sam with love in his voice, 'I will always be with you. Simply think of me, and I will be there. And, to make sure that I always know exactly what you want, I will show you a special way of talking to me.'

'I love you,' said Joseph, still looking deep into Sam's eyes.

'And I love you,' replied Sam, 'unconditionally, as I always have and always will. Remember, Joseph, we two are one.'

9. Joseph's Journal

The next morning Joseph awoke to the sound of his mother calling him for breakfast. 'It's on the table, hurry up or it'll get cold!'

'Was it a dream, or was it real?' he instantly asked himself. He gave a long stretching yawn, and that's when he noticed it. 'I feel different, still me, but now much more . . . more . . . what is this feeling?' he questioned, and peered around his bedroom. Everything was still the same, but he most definitely felt different. 'Could a dream, even a very wonderful dream, make me feel so different from how I felt before I went to sleep?' he asked himself, crawling out of bed.

Standing in front of the big wardrobe mirror he pulled his pyjama top over his head and a small sparkling cloud of golden thought-dust slipped from the pocket, and was sent shimmering through the air.

'I knew it wasn't a dream,' Joseph shouted in delight, as he caught some of the sparkling dust in his hand. In the twinkling of an eye, the golden thought-dust had fizzed and sparkled away into thin air, but he knew the memory of his adventure, and what he had learned, would always be with him.

Joseph tore down the stairs to breakfast feeling extra hungry. The next fifteen minutes were a blur of eating and frantic scribbling as he wrote notes and drawings in his big yellow journal about all the things he had learned, and the special way for talking to genies that Sam had shown him.

As Joseph walked to school that morning he felt like he was gliding. There was a spring in his step and he felt like he had a happy song playing inside of him. 'I feel,' he puzzled again to himself, '... more alive!' The realisation brought him to a stop in mid-stride. Everything and every-one around him seemed brighter and shinier, people looked happier – it was as if the whole world had a little more sparkle. Even people he hadn't really liked much seemed quite nice today.

Mrs Bagwalt was outside her front door picking up her milk from the doorstep when Joseph strolled by on his way to school. 'Good morning,' he said, wanting her to know that he didn't think she was a witch any more.

'Good morning to you,' said Mrs Bagwalt, with a smile so sweet that it made Joseph grin. 'She is a nice old lady,' he thought to himself walking through the school gates.

The day seemed much more interesting than usual and passed very quickly. During the breaks Joseph told Bob all about his adventure. He told him how everybody in the whole wide world has their very own genie to help them make things happen. He explained that thinking happy thoughts makes you happy, and thinking sad thoughts makes you sad. He even shared with him the magic words to make things happen, the words that everyone can use to command their own genie and work their own magic: the words 'I can'. And the part he enjoyed best of all, was sharing the magic of liking your self.

Every time Joseph said the magic words 'I Like My Self' or 'I Love My Self' a warm safe feeling swept through his insides and bubbled to his face in a beaming smile. And the more often he said it, the longer the feeling lasted.

Joseph got Bob to try saying the magic words himself, with as much feeling as possible and to notice the small warm glow that it gives you inside. 'And it gets stronger the more often you say it,' said Joseph as Bob smiled and giggled while saying 'I Like My Self'.

Joseph glided home feeling like he was still on the magic

carpet. He went into his house and was surprised to find his mother home early enjoying a nice cup of tea in the kitchen. Joseph proudly told her about his adventures and explained all he had learnt. Joseph wasn't sure whether she fully understood it all, but she had seemed interested. 'Never mind,' thought Joseph as he raced up the stairs towards his bedroom, 'maybe mum's genie will take her on a journey of understanding and then she'll know!'

In his bedroom he lay back on his bed and wondered about the last things Sam had said to him, 'Remember always, Joseph – the magic is inside of you! Everyone carries a little piece of magic inside. Use your magic by thinking and speaking words of happiness and you will be happy. You cannot control everything that happens, but you can always choose how to feel. Be a shining light and help other people to understand that they have magic too; so many people have forgotten, and their light grows low.

'Most of all, Joseph, remember Faith's key to set you free, see and say things as you want them to be.'

'Yes,' thought Joseph, 'magic thoughts, and magic words, make a magic me!' He slowly opened his eyes, took a deep happy breath, and spoke from his heart the greatest magic words of all, 'I Love My Self.'

Resources

Brian Mayne and his wife Sangeeta work to help people of all ages evolve their self and improve their lives. Their organisation, L.I.F.T. International, was founded on the following statement:

> *We are a community of Light leaders.*
> *We share Life Information For Transcendence*
> *in order to serve the evolution of humanity.*

Also available from Vermilion:

Life Mapping   ISBN 0-09-188455-1

Life Mapping is a unique personal empowerment technique designed to help you identify your life purpose and be the most magnificent you that you can be. Using a combination of ancient wisdom, timeless principles and accelerated learning, *Life Mapping* is simple to understand and fun to use, being both profound in its depth and great in its rewards.

Other L.I.F.T. International products and services available:

Joseph's Journal

A companion workbook to *Sam the Magic Genie* designed to capture the key lessons contained within the story of *Sam the Magic Genie* and then use them as a foundation for a powerful achievement technique called Goal-Mapping. Throughout history the most successful men and women have been those who have learned to develop the natural mental ability of goal setting. *Joseph's Journal* helps the user to gain this life skill early.

Goal-Mapping Surfers Guide

An easy-to-use guidebook walking you through the key steps to creating your Goal-Map. This handbook also features individual accounts and Goal-Maps to inspire and encourage you to create the life of your dreams.

Goal-Mapping Live (audio)

A 65-minute inspirational overview presentation on the power of positive focus and the success system of Goal-Mapping.

Goal-Mapping Pack (audio)

The pack consists of 6 audio-tapes and a 50-page workbook with practical exercises, examples and illustrations. Running time approx 4 hrs 30 mins.

For information about:

- any of the above products
- attending workshops and presentations
- education and teacher training
- keynote addresses to your organisation
- L.I.F.T. life-coaching services

contact L.I.F.T. International
Tel: +44 (0)1264 782543
www.liftinternational.com enquiries@liftinternational.com